# Hoagie's Rifle-Gun

# Hoagie's Rifle-Gun

by Miska Miles

Illustrated by John Schoenherr

An Atlantic Monthly Press Book

Little, Brown and Company   BOSTON   TORONTO

ATLANTIC–LITTLE, BROWN BOOKS
ARE PUBLISHED BY
LITTLE, BROWN AND COMPANY
IN ASSOCIATION WITH
THE ATLANTIC MONTHLY PRESS

*Published simultaneously in Canada
by Little, Brown & Company (Canada) Limited*

PRINTED IN THE UNITED STATES OF AMERICA

*To Brook Clymer*

The afternoon shadows were long, and the sun seemed to touch the hilltop.

In a deserted shack on the side of the hill, an old bobcat awakened and yawned widely. Silently, he moved across the broken floor.

On padded paws, he started out to hunt for his food.

3

In a small square house at the bottom of the hill, Hoagie sat on the edge of a bed and waited while his mother put the last stitches in a patch on his faded blue pants.

His young brother Ira leaned against the arm of their mother's chair.

"Hoagie didn't tear his pants," Ira said. "We were just walking along the path and it happened by itself. I saw it."

"Don't jiggle Ma's chair," Hoagie said. "Can't you see she's trying to hurry?"

When his mother had finished, she handed the pants to Hoagie.

Quickly he pulled them on.

"They're getting thin all over," his mother said.

"With that red patch," Ira said, "everybody can see where you're going."

It wasn't suppertime, but Hoagie was already thinking about supper. He thought about spareribs and corn bread and he swallowed hard.

"Seems like I'm always thinking about something to eat," Hoagie said.

"Maybe Pa will bring store food tonight," Ira said.

"Maybe so," their mother said. "I've been thinking all day that maybe he found work."

"But what if he didn't?" Hoagie asked. He thought about all those times when his father had come home, silent, solemn—those evenings when he sat on the porch, looking far off at nothing at all. "What if he didn't find work?"

His mother shook her head. "If he didn't, there's nothing to eat except the potatoes in the potato patch."

"Maybe I've got time to take the rifle-gun and scare up something for supper," Hoagie said. "Four o'clock plane just went over."

"Maybe you could try," his mother said.

Above the pegs where the rifle lay against the wall, a spider had neatly spun her web.

"Be careful and don't break that web, Hoagie," his mother said. "That spider web brings good luck." She looked in the little gray cardboard box where the bullets were kept. She pushed them around with a forefinger. "Not many left," she said.

"One bullet is all Hoagie needs," Ira said. "Hoagie never misses. Hoagie never wastes a bullet."

"I know," his mother said. She handed a bullet to Hoagie. "But first he has to find something to shoot at. And rabbits are getting harder and harder to find, because everybody around here has to hunt for food."

Hoagie loaded the rifle.

He was proud that he hadn't missed a target since he was ten years old, almost a year ago. He straightened his shoulders.

High on the hill, the bobcat hunted for his food.

Something moved in the brush. The bobcat crouched, his short tail twitched.

With one leap, he found his prey. But it was only a grasshopper. He ate it and silently stalked on through the brush.

The old bobcat had roamed these Cumberland Mountains for many years. Here, his only enemy was man.

In the small house far down at the bottom of
the hill, a door slammed and the smell of man
came with the wind.

The big cat climbed to the high safety of a
rocky ledge to wait and watch.

Quietly, Hoagie led the way along a narrow footpath, and Ira followed in his footsteps.

On they went, around and over an ugly pile of slag. When they were on the other side, Ira touched Hoagie's shirt.

"Look up," he said. "Look up there on the rocks. It's Old Bob. He's hungry. I wish I had something to give him."

"No matter what you left for him, Old Bob wouldn't take it," Hoagie said. "He doesn't like boy-smell."

"He likes me," Ira said. "Right now, he's looking straight at me. He's not even afraid. He knows I like him. I wish he wasn't hungry."

I'm as hungry as he is, Hoagie thought to himself. Hungrier, maybe.

"Hoagie, the first time you ever brought me hunting, you showed me Old Bob. He knows me."

"If he knows anybody, he knows me, too," said Hoagie, thinking of the time he first saw Old Bob. Pa had said, "Don't move. Look up there on the rocks. That's a bobcat. No cat'll bother you unless he's cornered. He's hunting. Same as we hunt. Take a good look. Not many bobcats left around here any more."

In the late afternoon sun, the bobcat's eyes flashed yellow.

"I've heard that a bobcat makes good eating if you're real hungry," Hoagie said.

"No," Ira said. "Pa said bobcat meat's not worth bringing home."

"I said it would be good eating if you're *real* hungry," Hoagie said.

"You wouldn't shoot Old Bob," Ira said.

"Well then, let's quit standing here looking at him and hunt for something for supper," Hoagie said. "And no more talking."

A rabbit scurried through the brush and disappeared before Hoagie could shoot.

"That was a big one," Ira said. "Why didn't you shoot?"

"I wasn't ready," Hoagie said. "I've got to be ready."

18

When the boys had gone ahead, the bobcat padded through the underbrush, watching for the flicker of a wood rat's ear or the whisk of a lizard's tail.

Beside the path, a weed quivered. The cat pounced.

Beneath his claws, the rabbit's feet kicked once and she was dead.

Leisurely, the old bobcat ate his supper.

Hoagie and Ira went on.

"Keep an eye out for that rabbit." Hoagie spoke softly. "We might still get her."

"By the rock—by the rock—" Ira said.

Hoagie lifted his gun.

"It's only a skinny little old ground squirrel. We'll get more than that for a meal." He lowered his rifle.

The sun was setting when Hoagie saw a movement beside the path. He pointed his gun.

A bull snake slithered through the weeds.

Ira laughed. "It's a good thing you didn't shoot that," he said. "Think what Ma would say if you took a bull snake home."

For another hour, they roamed over the hillside.

"Ma was right. Rabbits are hard to find. I should have been ready to shoot when we saw that big one," Hoagie said.

Below, in a swale of broom sedge and brambles, was the deserted shack. Its roof was full of holes and its porch was sagging.

"Let's look in the old shack," Ira said.

"We've looked there a hundred times," Hoagie said. "There's nothing in it except spiders and mice. It's getting late. Maybe Pa's home. We'd better go back."

They started for home. "Stay behind," Hoagie said. "We still might see something."

"Maybe we'll find a turkey gone to roost in a tree," Ira said. "Pa says there used to be wild turkeys around here."

"Used to be," Hoagie said.

They came to the place beside the path where the old bobcat had taken his supper.

"Look," Hoagie said. "The bobcat got that big rabbit. I know he did. Nothing else would make so much mess. I hate that cat. I hate him."

Ahead, the old bobcat climbed into an oak tree and sat comfortably in the fork of its branches.

26

Hoagie saw the cat in the tree. "Old Bob's up there," he said. "Stay where you are, Ira. Stand still." He lifted his rifle.

"You wouldn't shoot Old Bob," Ira said. "You wouldn't."

Hoagie leveled his gun.

"I won't *let* you shoot him." Ira pushed Hoagie's elbow.

Hoagie turned threateningly toward him. "Don't ever do that again. Don't touch me when I aim the rifle-gun."

"You wouldn't shoot Old Bob," Ira said.

I'll shoot him, Hoagie thought. He got my rabbit. I hate him.

He lifted his gun.

Ira threw himself on the ground and whimpered against the dirt.

Hoagie looked along the barrel of his rifle. He sighted exactly between the cat's eyes. He hardly heard Ira's sobbing.

As his fingers tensed on the trigger, the old bobcat looked straight at him. I can't do it, Hoagie thought. But it was too late.

He was shooting. The bullet zinged harmlessly over the bobcat's head. A puff of yellow dust rose from the slag pile beyond.

The bobcat jumped to the ground with grace and dignity and disappeared in the brush.

Ira was crying loudly.

"No use bawling," Hoagie said. "Old Bob is safe. We won't have meat tonight unless Pa worked today."

"I don't care," Ira said. "I'm not hungry." His face was streaked with dirt and tears.

32

"Wipe your face on your sleeve or everybody'll know you've been bawling," Hoagie said.

Ira wiped his face. "You *missed*. And I'm *glad*. You wasted a bullet."

Ira led the way home.

Their mother and father were sitting on the porch steps. Their father's hands were clasped loosely between his knees. He was looking at the ground.

"I see you didn't find anything," their mother said.

"Yes we did," Ira said. "We found something. And Hoagie missed."

Their father lifted his head slowly.

"Hoagie missed?" He sounded unbelieving. "How did you happen to miss, Hoagie?" he asked gently.

Hoagie set the butt of his rifle on the ground. He didn't want to answer.

"He shot at Old Bob," Ira said.

His father's shoulders drooped. "A boy has to be real hungry to shoot at a bobcat," he said.

Hoagie stood waiting.

"How did you happen to miss?" his father asked again. "Did you miss on purpose, Hoagie?"

"I don't know, Pa."

"Why don't you know?" his father asked mildly.

"Well," Hoagie said, "I aimed. I aimed right between his eyes. And just when I pulled the trigger, I knew I didn't want to kill him. And I missed."

"You know we have to hunt for food," his father said.

"I know. And I know why I didn't want to hit Old Bob. You can't shoot a thing when it isn't afraid of you."

"You can't shoot a thing when you know it by its name!" Ira said. "You just can't do it, Pa!"

Pa looked at the ground for a long time. He rubbed his forehead. Finally, Pa nodded slowly. "There's truth in what you say," he said.

Ma pushed herself up from the steps and went
inside the house.

Hoagie followed and set his rifle-gun carefully
on its pegs. The spider's web still swung there.

His mother lifted potatoes from the boiling
water and put them on plates.

"That's all there is," she said apologetically.

Pa shoved a chair to his place at the table.

"Tomorrow's different," he said. "I've got work for tomorrow. For one day. We'll have store food tomorrow night."

Ira lifted a large piece of potato with his fork. "I *like* potatoes," he said. "Hoagie and I—we like potatoes."

Up on the hill by the slag pile, the bobcat hunted for food. He was not hungry, but still he hunted—all night he hunted.

When morning came, he had found neither snake nor skunk. Quietly, he went downhill and through the broom sedge.

On he went, toward the deserted shack, where spiders waited in their dusty webs, where mice scampered over the broken floor.